For the Children
Pam, Randy, Rick, Aundrea, Michael, Tim,
Jodi, Christopher, Jenny, Jeremy, Jeanne, Annie,
Holly, Colby, Dallas, Savannah,

Bansari
and your name here

*A special thanks to
Miss Margaret H. Kling*

Babes in Toyland

Retold and illustrated by
Toby Bluth

Adapted from the operetta by
Victor Herbert and Glen Macdonough

CHILDRENS PRESS, CHICAGO®
School & Library Edition

ISBN 0-516-09176-X

When you've
grown up, my dears
And are as old as I
You'll often ponder on the years
that roll so swiftly by,

And of the many lands
You will have journeyed through
You'll oft recall the best of all,
The land your childhood knew!

Toyland, Toyland!
Little girl and boy land,
While you dwell within it
You are ever happy then.

Childhood's joyland,
mystic merry toyland!
Once you pass its portals,
You can ne'er return again.

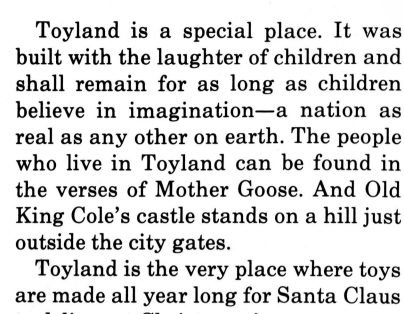

Toyland is a special place. It was built with the laughter of children and shall remain for as long as children believe in imagination—a nation as real as any other on earth. The people who live in Toyland can be found in the verses of Mother Goose. And Old King Cole's castle stands on a hill just outside the city gates.

Toyland is the very place where toys are made all year long for Santa Claus to deliver at Christmastime.

There was a master toymaker who had a large workshop where most of the people in town worked. They worked very hard from sunrise to sun-set. But when work is playing with

toys all day long, then work can seem a whole lot more like fun. That was just how the people of Toyland viewed their situation.

The master toymaker's chief assistant was a bright, young lad named Tom-Tom, the Piper's son. Tom was clever and artistic. Where another might make a toy that is just a toy, Tom's toys seemed almost alive.

One day an unusual order came from Santa for one hundred wooden soldiers, six feet tall.

"Now that is a tall order," said the master toymaker. "The best person to make these soldiers is my assistant, Tom-Tom."

When Tom had completed his soldiers, everyone in Toyland was impressed— even Tom. "Yes," he said to himself, "I am a clever fellow."

There was another man in Toyland who considered himself very clever. His name was Barnaby.

Unfortunately, in the best of all possible worlds, which this was, there are some people who are not the best of all possible people, which Mr. Barnaby wasn't.

He was a miserly old skinflint. He hoarded what he had and coveted what he did not. He could quickly tell you the price of everything in Toyland, but he never understood the value of any of it. He never laughed. He never cried. And his eyes were as cold as the gold he hid inside his dark little house.

Mr. Barnaby spent his life getting people in his debt. Then he would make it impossible for them to pay, and he would claim for himself whatever such people might own.

Secretly he hoped one day to own Toyland. Then, all the people in Toyland would work just for him, and not for Santa Claus.

Mr. Barnaby had taken two orphan children into his home. Their names were Alan and Jane. He claimed they were his nephew and niece, and to prove it, he produced a letter from their late parents stating that Mr. Barnaby was the children's uncle. Since the letter seemed real, Old King Cole decreed that Alan and Jane should live with Barnaby.

But the letter was a fake written by Mr. Barnaby himself. Alan's and Jane's parents had left the children a fortune. Mr. Barnaby wanted that money.

Mr. Barnaby treated Alan and Jane badly. He dressed them only in rags and patches and fed them mostly stale bread and water. But worst of all, when he lost his temper, which was often, he beat them!

Fortunately, Tom-Tom, the Piper's son, took Alan and Jane under his wing. Tom had never liked Mr. Barnaby and he didn't trust him. He didn't believe Alan and Jane were really Mr. Barnaby's nephew and niece. He was going to watch over them until he found out what Barnaby was up to.

The new babes needed friends, so Tom introduced them to Mother Hubbard's children.

"Listen, everybody," he said. "I want you to meet Alan and Jane."

"Hello," said Simple Simon, who had just come back from fishing. "Welcome to Toyland. This little girl with the curl right in the middle of her forehead is my sister Mary, Mary Quite Contrary."

Mary's younger brother Wee Willie Winkie added, "And when she is good, she is very, very good."

Her other brother Jack Be Nimble, Jack Be Quick said, "But when she is bad, she is horrid!"

Just then Little Boy Blue came running and blowing his horn. "Hey, everybody!" he hollered, "Bo Peep is in trouble."

"What's the trouble?" asked Tom.

"She's lost her sheep," answered Little Boy Blue, "and she doesn't know where to find them."

"Tell her not to worry," said Tom. "We'll find her sheep."

Tom and the children hunted all over Toyland for the sheep. Suddenly Alan heard noises.

Ba! Ba! Ba!

"The sound is coming from Mr. Barnaby's yard!" said Jane.

Tom came running. Sure enough, there, locked in Barnaby's backyard, were the lost sheep.

"Barnaby," exclaimed Tom. "This is just the kind of thing he would do!"

Tom, Alan, and Jane took the lost sheep back to Bo Peep.

"Oh, Tom," said Bo Peep, "how clever of you to find them."

Tom thought to himself that this would be the perfect moment to ask Bo Peep to be his sweetheart. But he was too shy, so instead he just said, "I didn't do it alone. It was Alan and Jane who heard them first."

"Alan and Jane!" said a familiar voice. It was Mr. Barnaby and he was angry.

"I'm pleased you found your sheep, Miss Peep," he said. "I'm sorry to say they have caused considerable damage to my yard. You will, of course, pay me for the damages."

"But Mr. Barnaby," said Bo Peep, "how can I ever pay you?"

"Quite simple, my pet," he replied. "When you shear your sheep of their wool, you can give me three bags full. That should take care of it nicely."

Tom was getting angry.

"But Mr. Barnaby," pleaded Bo Peep. "My mother is a widow who lives in a shoe. You are our landlord. The wool pays for our rent."

"You would never have to worry about the rent on your shoe," said Mr. Barnaby, moving uncomfortably close to the young girl, "if you would marry me."

Tom lost control. He knocked Mr. Barnaby to the ground.

"You'll regret this!" threatened Barnaby. "Alan, Jane, get me home," he ordered.

The frightened babes did not dare disobey.

When they got home, the children were expecting the worst. Instead, to their surprise, Mr. Barnaby brought out two presents.

"Go ahead. Open them," he coaxed.

The children opened their presents. Inside were brand new clothes—two little sailor suits with black ties and shiny, new shoes. They were both confused. Mr. Barnaby had never been nice to them before.

"Early tomorrow you are going on a picnic," began Barnaby. "Two friends of mine, who are very fine sailors, will take you for a ride in their boat. Now, off to bed you go."

Later that night when Alan and Jane were in their beds, they could not sleep. In spite of their new clothes and tomorrow's picnic, they both felt something was wrong. Alan and Jane were scared.

The poor babes—how could they know that Mr. Barnaby's two sailors were really two pirates named Roderigo and Gonzorgo. Mr. Barnaby had paid them to take the children out in their boat and drown them. Then he would get their money.

"Alan," said Jane, "I hear singing."

"Me, too," said Alan.

They got out of their beds and flung open the window. Toyland was flooded with moonlight.

"The singing is coming from Mother Hubbard's shoe. It's Tom-Tom," said Jane. "It's Tom-Tom singing to Little Bo Peep."

"I guess he had to sing," said Alan. "He's too shy to talk. Look, there are the kids. There are Mother Hubbard's kids."

Simple Simon, Contrary Mary, Wee Willie Winkie, Jack Be Nimble, and Little Boy Blue were providing the chorus for Tom's love song.

The song was so sweet that the children forgot their fears. Alan and Jane fell asleep in each other's arms there in the window.

The next day was important for Tom-Tom. Santa had arrived at the master toymaker's workshop to inspect the progress of the toys. He brought with him a flask filled with a strange light.

"I want you to keep this in a safe place," he told the master toymaker.

"What is it?" asked Tom.

"It's a lot of bad thoughts," said Santa. "I have gathered them from the outside world. Believe me, it will be better without them. Now, let's see the toys."

Tom was eager to show Santa his life-sized toy soldiers. If Santa is pleased, thought Tom, this could mean a promotion or a bonus or a raise—maybe all three! Then he could pay the mortgage on Mother Hubbard's shoe. Mr. Barnaby would never be able to bother Mother Hubbard, her children, or Little Bo Peep again.

Santa was more than happy with everything he saw. Now it was Tom's big moment.

Tom brought out the soldiers. Santa was stunned.

"What is this?" he asked.

"It's the toy soldiers you ordered," beamed Tom. "One hundred toy soldiers, six feet tall."

Santa started to chuckle. Then he laughed. Then he roared so hard that the tears rolled down his cheeks.

"Ho! Ho! Ho!" Santa gasped. "No! No! No! You've got it all mixed up. I didn't order one hundred soldiers, six feet tall. I ordered six hundred soldiers, one foot tall. Ho! Ho! Ho!"

Tom's heart sank. How could he have made so costly a mistake?

The master toymaker helped Santa back to his sleigh. When he returned, he told Tom he was fired.

Tom went for a long walk. He didn't want to see anyone or talk to anyone. He was sure Santa had ordered one hundred toy soldiers, six feet tall. He remembered commenting on how large a toy that would make when Mr. Barnaby gave him the order.

Mr. Barnaby! That was it! Mr. Barnaby had deliberately changed the order to get Tom fired! Well, he had gone too far this time!

Tom was headed for Barnaby's house when he

heard Little Bo Peep.

"Tom! Tom!" she cried. "Alan and Jane are missing, and there are two sailors in town telling people they saw you drown them."

"It's not true!" cried Tom.

Just then Mr. Barnaby came down the street with Roderigo and Gonzorgo. "That's him," he shouted. "Seize him."

The pirates grabbed Tom, but he broke free.

"Run, Tom, run!" cried Bo Peep.

Tom fled as fast as his feet would carry him.

The Hubbard children joined Bo Peep. "We saw him," they said. "He got away."

"Which is more than you will do," fumed Barnaby. "Either you consent to marry me tomorrow, Miss Peep, or your entire family will be flung into the street tonight!"

"But Mr. Barnaby," she wept, "I don't love you."

"Who said anything about love?" said Barnaby, kissing her trembling hand.

"Mr. Barnaby," sobbed the girl, "you are wicked and hateful."

"Yes, I know," smiled Mr. Barnaby, "but you'll be surprised at how attractive money can make me."

When Tom finally stopped running, he was well beyond Toyland. He sat down exhausted to figure out what to do next. Then he noticed something poking its little fuzzy face out from behind a rock. It was a cinnamon brown baby bear. The bear smiled at Tom. Tom smiled at the bear.

"Hello," he said to the bear. "It sure is nice to see a friendly face."

Fuzzy Bear rolled around on the ground, inviting Tom to play.

"I don't feel much like playing," Tom explained. "I just heard that my two friends Alan and Jane drowned. I think it was done by a couple of pirates," he added.

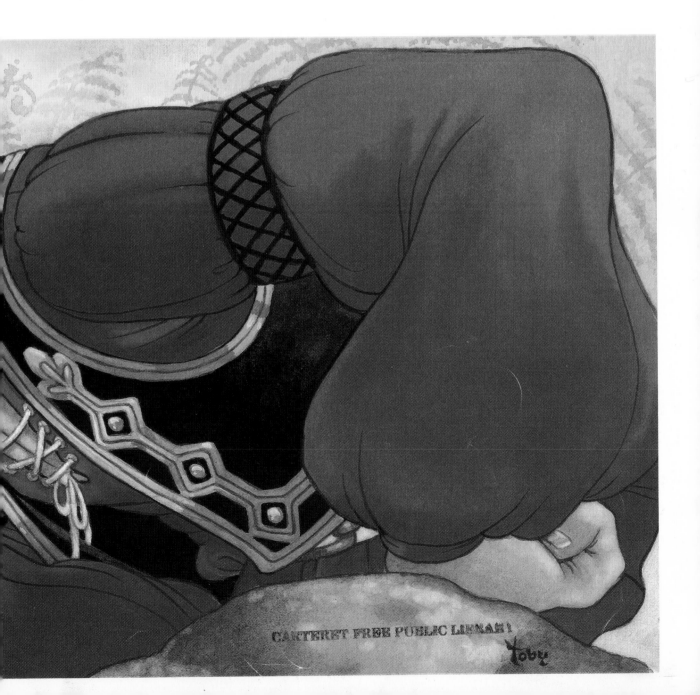

Fuzzy shook his head no. He took Tom's hand in his paw and led him through the woods to a gypsy camp. There were Alan and Jane, tied up with a rope, but still very much alive, and guarded by an old gypsy hag. Instead of drowning the babes, the greedy Roderigo and Gonzorgo sold them to the gypsies. On a stool near Alan and Jane was a beautiful white butterfly imprisoned in a bottle.

"You've got to help me," Tom said.

Fuzzy nodded his head yes, then he and Tom quietly tiptoed to Alan and Jane. Carefully, they untied the ropes. Jane opened the jar on the stool, setting the butterfly free. Just then, the hag spotted them.

"Thieves!" she shrieked. "Thieves! After them!"

A band of wild gypsies appeared with knives flashing!

"Run," shouted Tom. And they all ran.

"Faster!" shouted the hag to her cronies. "Don't let them get away!"

"Don't look back!" ordered Tom. "Just keep running and stay together!"

Fuzzy Bear growled his most ferocious growl, but he was such a little bear, that it had little effect upon the pursuing gypsies.

"I paid good money for those brats!" screamed the hag. "I am being cheated, cheated!"

"They're getting closer!" cried Jane.

"Run ahead!" shouted Tom. "I'll try to hold them off!"

Fuzzy stayed by Tom's side, his growl sounding fiercer all the time.

"When I catch you," threatened the hag, "I'll skin you alive and rub you with salt!"

"I can't run any farther," sobbed Jane.

"You've got to," said Alan, taking her hand and pulling her along.

They came to a deep, dark forest. "Into the forest," ordered Tom. "Maybe we can hide in there."

The babes, Fuzzy, Tom, and the butterfly darted into the forest. Tom spotted a hollow log. They all crawled inside, scarcely daring to breathe. Then they waited to see what would happen.

The band of gypsies stopped at the edge of the forest. From inside the log, Tom and the children could hear them.

"You blundering fools," howled the hag. "You've run into the Forest of No Return. You may not be mine, but you'll never find your way home. No one has ever come back from the Forest of No Return." And the gypsies left.

Tom, Alan, Jane, and Fuzzy crept cautiously out of the log. The butterfly fluttered after.

"Fuzzy," asked Tom, "have you ever heard of this Forest of No Return?"

Fuzzy nodded his head yes.

"And, is it really true that anyone who goes in, never comes out?"

The bear nodded again.

"Are we going to die?" asked Alan.

"No," said Tom. "We are not going to die."

"I'm frightened," said Jane, struggling to hold back her tears.

"There, there, now," Tom said. "Don't be afraid. I'm not sure what we're going to do, but everything is going to be all right. Let's get a good night's sleep. Things will look brighter in the morning."

The babes and the bear lay down on the soft, warm moss. Tom stood watch so that nothing could harm them. He sang a lullaby and soon they were fast asleep.

Then, a very strange thing happened. The beautiful white butterfly began to glow. Hundreds of other glowing butterflies from all over the forest came.

Tom was not sure what was happening. He woke the babes and the bear. Then, right before their eyes, the butterflies turned into fairies, and the white butterfly was transformed into the queen of the fairies.

The shimmering fairy court descended to the ground. The babes, the bear, and Tom were all speechless.

"It was very kind of you to free me from the gypsies," spoke the fairy queen. "And now, it's my turn to help you. Bring me some dewdrops," she said to her fairy court.

Instantly, the fairies brought great armloads of sparkling dew. They placed them before the fairy queen. She waved her wand and the dewdrops turned to gold. "This," she said, "will pay the mortgage on Mother Hubbard's shoe."

"How did you know about Mother Hubbard's shoe?" asked Tom.

"We fairies know many things that mortals find hard to understand," she answered. "We even know how to get you out of the Forest of No Return."

"You do!" squealed Alan and Jane.

"Yes, listen."

TOOT! TOOT! came the sound of a whistle.

"That's the Toyland Express returning from the North Pole. Mortals may not know the way out of the forest, but the train just follows its tracks."

"Let's hurry," shouted Tom. "We've got to catch a train."

They ran toward the sound of the whistle. They flagged down the train and climbed on board.

Tom spoke to the engine, "Can you take us out of the Forest of No Return and back to Toyland?"

TOOT! TOOT! "I think I can."

Down the track, clickety-clack, sped the little engine that could, singing all the way, "I think I can, I think I can, I think I can."

Back in Toyland, Mr. Barnaby heard that Tom, Alan, and Jane had returned. He heard about their bag of gold. He would not get Mother Hubbard's shoe. He would not get Alan and Jane's money, and he would not get Bo Peep. Barnaby wanted revenge.

He went to the master toymaker's workshop. He took the flask of evil thoughts Santa had captured.

If he could not have Toyland for himself, no one else could have it either. He pulled the cork. Thoughts poured forth, slowly transforming themselves into a legion of monstrous boogies.

"Now, my pets," smiled Barnaby. "We will tear Toyland down."

Barnaby and the boogies descended on Toyland.

The people of Toyland were caught by surprise, but they fought back bravely to save their town. They were far outnumbered. The boogies were winning! It would take a miracle now to save Toyland.

Then, like a flash of light, Tom was struck with an inspiration. "Come with me," he said to the Hubbard children.

Tom and the children fought their way to the master toymaker's workshop. Breathless, they burst through the door. There before them stood 100 toy soldiers, six feet tall!

"Wind them up!" ordered Tom.

Simon, Jack, Mary, Willie, Alan, Jane, and Fuzzy Bear quickly wound the keys in the backs of the wooden soldiers.

"Boy Blue!" ordered Tom, "Blow your horn!"

Little Boy Blue raised his trumpet and blew once. Ta-Ta...Ta-Ta. The soldiers snapped to attention!

He blew twice. Ta-Ta...Ta-Ta...Ta-Ta... Ta-Ta. The toys shouldered their candy cane rifles.

Ta-Ta...Ta-Ta...Ta-Ta...Ta-Ta...Ta-Ta...- Ta-Ta...a drumroll and they advanced.

Out the door of the master toymaker's workshop marched Tom-Tom, the Piper's son, the Babes of Toyland, and an army of 100 toy soldiers, six feet tall.

The people of Toyland cheered when they saw them coming. Their faint hearts grew strong again. They battled the boogies with renewed courage and determination. Back they drove them ...back... back...to the portals of Toyland. The boogies fled out of the gates and into the outside world where they vanished. They had become, once again, only bad thoughts for Santa and grown-ups to deal with.

Mr. Barnaby was seized with fear. He turned a cowardly yellow and ran far away, never to be seen again.

Toyland was saved, thanks to Tom-Tom.

Little Bo Peep threw her arms around his neck and kissed her hero. This set the babes to whistling and cheering. Simon leaped into the air, clicking his heels together several times. Jack jumped back and

forth over his candlestick. Wee Willie and Fuzzy shouted, while Little Boy Blue blew his horn. Alan and Jane hugged him gratefully. Contrary Mary was so happy, she cried.

Toyland is still here today. It hasn't changed and probably never will. It's that little girl and boy land in every child, no matter how old he may be.